DiNo

Pete Can Fly!

by Bonnie Williams • illustrated by John Gordon

Ready-to-Read

Simon Spotlight
New York   London   Toronto   Sydney   New Delhi

SIMON SPOTLIGHT
An imprint of Simon & Schuster Children's Publishing Division
1230 Avenue of the Americas, New York, New York 10020
For information about special discounts for bulk purchases, please contact Simon & Schuster
Special Sales at 1-866-506-1949 or business@simonandschuster.com.
Manufactured in the United States of America 0614 LAK
First Edition
10 9 8 7 6 5 4 3 2 1
Library of Congress Cataloging-in-Publication Data
Williams, Bonnie.
Pete can fly! / by Bonnie Williams ; illustrated by John Gordon. — First edition.
pages cm. — (Ready-to-read) (Dino School)
Summary: "Teddy the T. rex is jealous that his best friend Pete the Pterodactyl can fly.
But when a friend Tina the Triceratops reminds Teddy of all the great things a T. rex can do,
Teddy ends up feeling much better about himself."— Provided by publisher.
ISBN 978-1-4814-0465-5 (pbk) — ISBN 978-1-4814-0466-2 (hc)— ISBN 978-1-4814-0467-9 (eBook)
[1. Tyrannosaurus rex—Fiction. 2. Pterodactyls—Fiction. 3. Dinosaurs—Fiction.
4. Self-acceptance—Fiction.] I. Gordon, John, 1967- illustrator. II. Title.
PZ7.W655872Pe 2014
[E]—dc23
2014000870

Teddy the Tyrannosaurus rex
and Pete the Pterodactyl
are best friends.

They do everything together.

They swing on the swings.

They slide down the slide.

They seesaw on the seesaw.

Today they are playing
kickball.

Val the Velociraptor
kicks the ball.

The ball goes high.

Teddy cannot reach it. . . .

Pete can!

Pete can fly.

Pete catches the ball.

Everyone cheers for Pete!

It is time for class.
"Today I will show you
a map of the world,"
says Ms. G.

"It is a big place with
many different dinosaurs."

Ms. G. tries to pull down
the map.
She cannot reach it.
Can anyone help?

Pete can!

Pete can fly.

Pete pulls down the map.

Everyone cheers for Pete!

After school,
Tina the Triceratops
sees a big cloud in the sky.
"I hope it is not going to
rain," she says.

Pete flies up to the cloud

for a better look.

When he returns he says,

"It is not a rain cloud."

Everyone cheers for Pete!

"Pete is cool," says Tina.

"He can fly!"

Teddy is sad. He is not cool.

He cannot fly.

Tina does not want Teddy
to feel sad.
She knows he can do lots of
cool things.

"You can run really fast,"
says Tina.

"And your tail makes the best rope for jumping over."

"Your roar is the loudest of all," adds Val.

Teddy smiles.

His friends are right.

He cannot fly,

but he can do lots of

other cool things!

"And there is one more
thing," adds Pete.

"Just because you cannot
fly like me,
does not mean you cannot
fly with me!"

Whee!